W9-CFB-155

MAY WHITNEY

EBR   ZOL   c.1
Zolotow, Charlotte,1915-
The old dog /

3 3117 0011 0758

DISCARDED

MAY WHITNEY
SCHOOL LIBRARY

THE OLD DOG

MAY WHITNEY
SCHOOL LIBRARY.

by Charlotte Zolotow   paintings by James Ransome

HarperCollinsPublishers

For CHARLOTTE CLARE BURKE
with much love
—Charlotte

In memory of
ROY LaGRONE—
Tuskegee Airman, Illustrator, Designer,
first African-American Member of the Society of Illustrators
and a wonderful person who will be missed by all who knew him.
—J.R.

The Old Dog

Text copyright © 1972 by Sarah Abbott, 1995 by Charlotte Zolotow

Illustrations copyright © 1995 by James Ransome

Printed in Mexico. All rights reserved.

Library of Congress Cataloging-in-Publication Data

Zolotow, Charlotte, 1915-

    The old dog / by Charlotte Zolotow ; paintings by James Ransome. — Rev. and
newly illustrated ed.

       p.   cm.

    Summary: When a young boy finds his old dog dead one morning, he spends the
rest of the day thinking about all the good times they had together.

    ISBN 0-06-024409-7. – ISBN 0-06-024412-7 (lib. bdg.)

    [1. Dogs—Fiction.   2. Pets—Fiction.   3. Death—Fiction.   4. Grief—Fiction.]

I. Ransome, James, ill. II. Title.

PZ7.Z77Ol 1995   93-41081

[E]—dc20   CIP

                                                    AC

Typography by Christine Kettner

3 4 5 6 7 8 9 10

❖

Revised and Newly Illustrated Edition

THE OLD DOG

Ben went to pat his
dog good morning.
She didn't open her eyes.
She was an old dog.

He patted her,
but she didn't wag her tail.

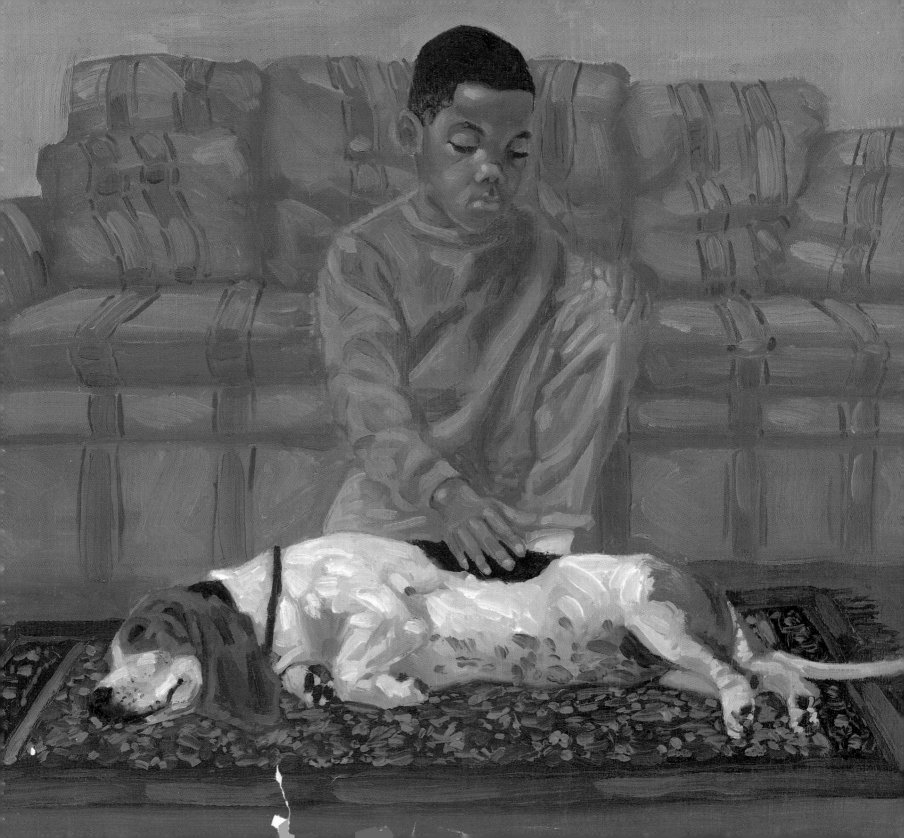

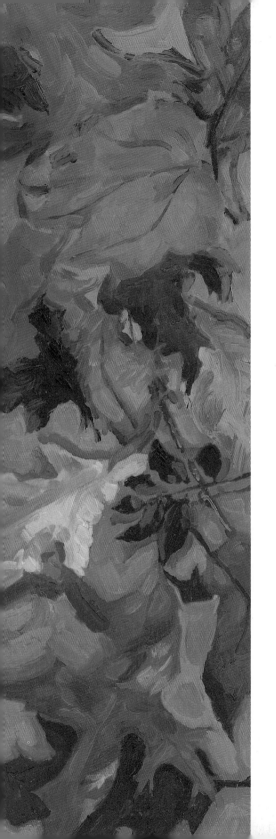

Ben got his father.

His father leaned over the old dog.

He shook his head slowly
and put his arm around Ben.
"She's dead," he said softly.

Ben looked at his dog,
but she didn't look back.
She just lay still.
Ben didn't understand.

He walked to school slowly,
and when he came home,
old dog wasn't at the door
to meet him.
Ben drank his milk,
but old dog was not there
watching him.

He went outside
and ran down the hill,
the way he and old dog always did,
but old dog wasn't there
to run with him.

He picked up a good stick,
but there was no one to throw it for.
Ben went back up the hill
and into the house.

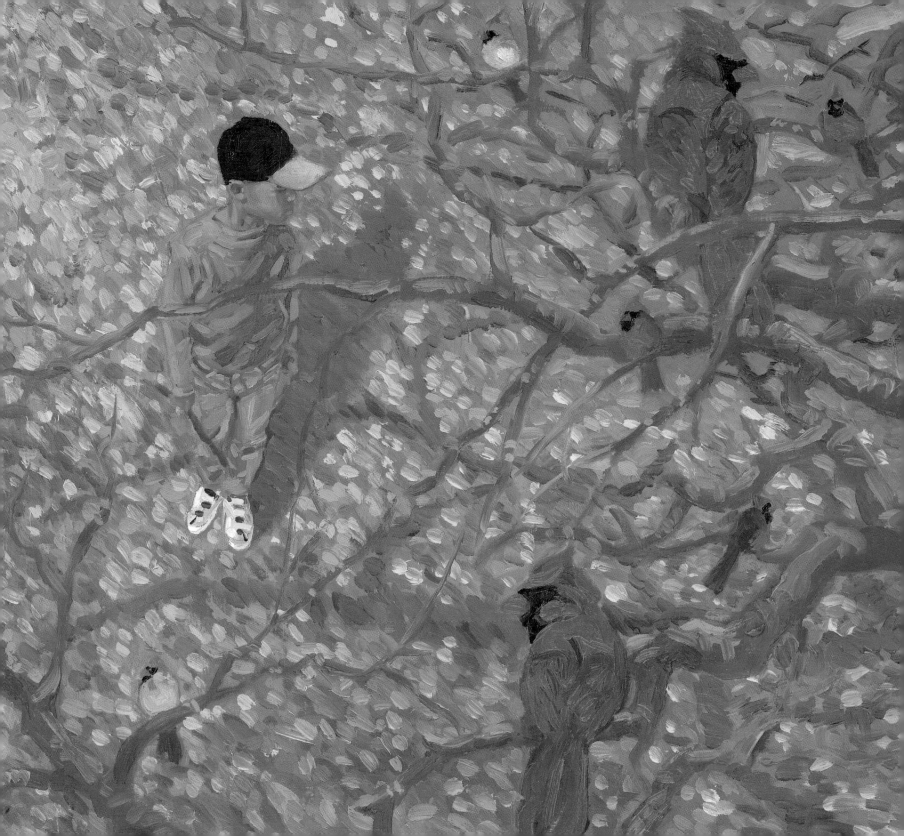

When the phone rang,
no big dog came rushing
to bark at the sound.

Ben went over to the window.

He stared outside.

"Death means someone isn't there,"
he thought.

He was very lonely.

It would never be the same.

He closed his eyes
and almost saw old dog.

"I miss you,"

he said into the air.

He began to cry.

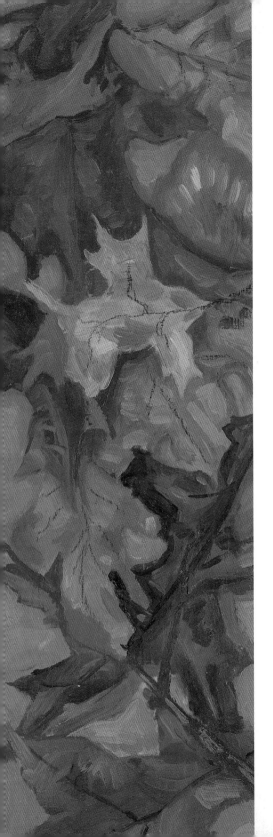

No old brown-and-white dog
was there to comfort him . . .

or to welcome

the new white-and-black puppy

Ben's father was bringing home.